PARADE DAY

Marching through the Calendar Year

Bob Barner

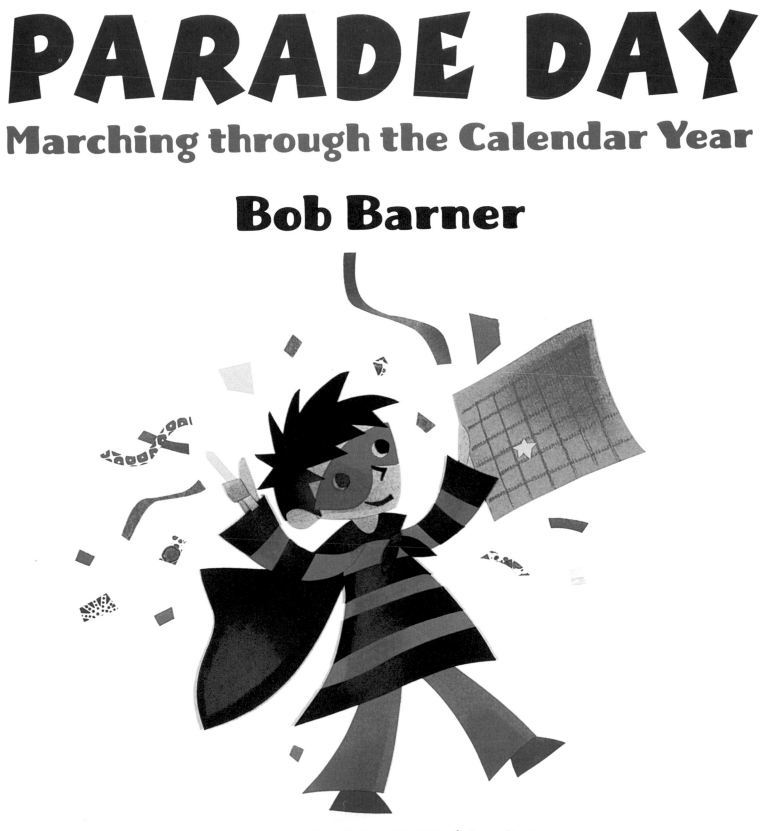

HOLIDAY HOUSE / New York

The collage art was made with cut and torn paper collected from all over the world, fabric, and pastels.
The text typeface is Kosmik Bold Two.

Library of Congress Cataloging-in-Publication Data
Barner, Bob.
Parade day: marching through the calendar year / Bob Barner.—1st ed.
p. cm.
Summary: Easy rhyming text describes a parade celebrating each month
of the year, followed by information about different calendars, the months,
and how to make one's own calendar.
ISBN 0-8234-1690-9 (hardcover)
[1. Parades—Fiction. 2. Months. 3. Calendar. 4. Stories in rhyme.] I. Title.
PZ8.3.B25213 Par 2003
[E]—dc21
2002068916

To Joan Stevenson, who loves a parade

January 1 begins a new calendar year.

Watch the Rose Bowl Parade and give a big cheer.

February Winter Carnival is filled with ice and snow.

Wear your scarf and mittens to this frosty show.

March 17 is the Saint Patrick's Day Parade.

Wear the color green on this lucky Irish day.

In a ticker tape parade in April, confetti fills the sky.

Cheer for our heroes as they pass by.

Dance to mariachi music on the fifth day of May.
Celebrate a Mexican festival at the Cinco de Mayo Parade.

Brush your cocker spaniel. Tie your bunny with a bow.

A pet parade in June is a happy, furry show.

On July 4 we wave flags and say hurray.

Wear red, white, and blue on Independence Day.

Animals parade in August when the circus is in town.

Elephants and ponies follow a circus clown.

The first Monday of September is the Labor Day Parade.

Everyone can come because there is no school today.

Dress up in your costume and trick-or-treat tonight.

On the thirty-first of October you may see a spooky sight.

Look for giant balloons floating high today.

On the fourth Thursday of November watch the Thanksgiving Day Parade.

On December 25 Santa rides in his sleigh.

Eight tiny reindeer pull him in the Christmas Parade.

January

January is the first month of a new year. There are 31 days in January. The first day of this month is called New Year's Day. The Rose Bowl Parade takes place in Pasadena, California, every New Year's Day. The floats are covered with real flowers. Martin Luther King, Jr. Day is observed on the third Monday in January. Chinese New Year is celebrated in January or February. Parades with lion dancers and dragons are said to bring people good luck in the new year.

February

February is the second month of the year. There are usually 28 days in this month. Every four years February has an extra day called Leap Day. Groundhog Day is on February 2. Valentine's Day is on February 14. Presidents' Day is on the third Monday of the month. In February or March, Mardi Gras is celebrated in cities and towns in Louisiana with festivals and parades.

March

March is the third month of the year. There are 31 days in this month. March 17 is St. Patrick's Day. It is a custom to wear green on this day. Easter parades take place on Easter Sunday in either March or April.

July

July is the seventh month of the year, and it is 31 days long. We celebrate our Independence Day on the fourth of July. Many towns across the United States have Fourth of July parades.

August

August has 31 days and is the eighth month of the year. Friendship Day is on August 2.

September

September has 30 days and is the ninth month of the year. The first Monday of September is Labor Day. The Jewish New Year, Rosh Hashanah, falls in September or October.

April

April has 30 days. It is the fourth month of the year. The first day of this month is April Fool's Day.

May

May is the fifth month of the year. There are 31 days in this month. Cinco de Mayo, which means the "fifth of May" in Spanish, is a Mexican festival filled with music, food, and dancing. We celebrate Mother's Day on the second Sunday in May. Memorial Day is observed on the last Monday of the month.

June

June has 30 days and is the sixth month of the year. Father's Day comes on the third Sunday in June. School summer vacation often starts during this month.

October

October has 31 days and is the tenth month of the year. Columbus Day falls on the second Monday of October. The last day of October is Halloween. New York City has a large Halloween Parade. Your neighborhood may have a parade at school or inside at the shopping center.

November

November has 30 days and is the eleventh month of the year. Members of the armed forces are honored on the eleventh of November, Veterans Day. The fourth Thursday of November is Thanksgiving Day. Every year there is a huge Thanksgiving Day Parade in New York City filled with giant balloons and marching bands.

December

December has 31 days and is the twelfth and last month of the year. Christmas Day comes on December 25. Some cities and towns have a Christmas Day Parade or a ceremony to light the official Christmas tree. Hanukkah usually falls in December. Kwanzaa begins on December 26.

MAKE YOUR OWN CALENDAR

Make your own calendar to remind you of special days, such as your birthday, when your vacation starts, or any other days you don't want to forget. Choose a month that is special to you and follow these directions to make a simple calendar for a month. You may want to have an adult help you.

Find the month you have chosen on a new calendar. You will need to use it as a guide.

First draw six horizontal lines across the paper that are an equal distance apart. You can use a ruler to measure.

Write the name of your month at the top of the sheet.

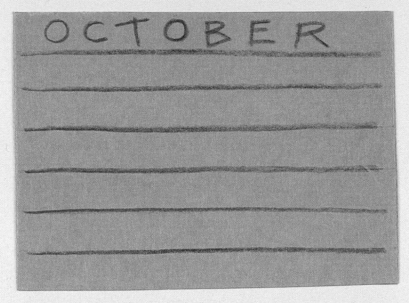

Next draw six lines that are vertical and the same space apart. This will give you seven sections across for the 7 days of the week. List the days of the week at the top of each box beginning with Sunday.

Check the calendar you are using as a guide to see which day begins the month. Number the days starting with the number 1 and ending with 28, 29, 30, or 31.

Put your calendar on the wall or on the refrigerator with a magnet. Check it every day to see when your next special day is coming up. You can make calendars for the other 11 months and have a calendar for the whole year.

Color in your special days with markers or colored pencil, or decorate them with stickers, rubber stampings, glitter, or drawings. Print your special information in the blocks. Every day that passes can be crossed off with a mark, so you can keep track of your month.

CALENDAR INFORMATION

Most calendars used today are Gregorian calendars. Named for Pope Gregory XIII in 1582, this calendar has 365 days and a leap year, every fourth year, with 366 days.

In our calendar 1 day equals the amount of time it takes Earth to turn on its axis. One year is equal to the amount of time it takes Earth to orbit the sun. Our calendar is divided into 12 months containing 52 weeks, for a total of 365 days. Each week has 7 days: five weekdays and 2 weekend days.

Every fourth year has an extra day in February. These years with 366 days are called leap years. Our calendar changes every year. Your birthday may be on a Saturday when you turn six but on a Sunday when you turn seven.

All calendars aren't like ours.

The Chinese calendar has 12 months based on the moon, 6 with 29 days and 6 with 30 days. There are 24 periods of 15 days each named for changing seasons. One of them, The Walking of Insects, begins in March. Chinese New Year is usually in January or February.

The Jewish calendar figures days by the sun and months by the moon. The 12 months alternate between 29 and 30 days. Rosh Hashanah, the Jewish New Year, is celebrated in the fall.

The Islamic calendar has 354 days and months with 29 or 30 days. A new day begins at sunset. During the ninth month of the Islamic year, Muslims observe Ramadan. While observing Ramadan, Muslims fast during the day and spend less time on everyday things so they can concentrate on worship.

There are several Hindu calendars. Most of them have 12 months that have 27 to 31 days each. Each month is measured from full moon to full moon and divided into a dark half and a bright half.

The Buddhist calendar calculates the year by the position of the sun in relation to the 12 segments of the heavens, each named for a sign of the zodiac.

Learn this rhyme to remember the number of days in each month.

Thirty days hath September,
April, June, and November;
All the rest have thirty-one,
Excepting February alone,
And that has twenty-eight days clear
And twenty-nine each leap year.